A Canadian Child's Year

SUNFLAKES & SNOWSHINE

by Fran Newman and Claudette Boulanger

with an afterword by Sheila Egoff

North Winds Press

A division of Scholastic-TAB Publications Ltd., Richmond Hill, Ontario, Canada design by Kathryn Cole

Published by North Winds Press, a division of Scholastic-TAB Publications Ltd.,
123 Newkirk Rd., Richmond Hill, Ontario, Canada

This edition, created to commemorate the International Year of the Child 1979,
is based on an original paperback edition published in 1977.

1st printing 1979   **Printed in Canada**

Canadian Cataloguing in Publication Data

Newman, Fran, 1937–
    Sunflakes & snowshine

Poems.

ISBN 0-590-07622-1

I. Boulanger, Claudette, 1940–   II. Title.

PS8577.E963S85   jC811′.5′4   C79-094043-4
PZ7.N48Su

I'm glad I don't live
Where it's sun and rain,
Then sun
And rain
Again, again!

I'm glad that I live
Where there's ice and snow,
And fall
And spring
And summer glow.

I'm glad that I live
Where seasons change;
I like
My world
To rearrange!

January

in darkened hours
frost
began to paint
my window glass

the morning sun
shone
through icy blooms —
light wisp of grass

a frozen scene
lit
with fiery warmth —
snow buds unfold

January

Brand-new skates,
Wintry day;
Take one step,
Feet give way!

Skis all set,
Hill too steep;
Down I fall
In a heap!

Toboggan ready,
On I hop;
I roll off,
It won't stop!

Winter sports
Have lost appeal;
I'll stay in
Until I heal!

February

Old Man Winter
is icing up my toes,
shivering my shoulders,
reddening my nose.

Old Man Winter
is watering my eyes,
nibbling at my fingers,
feet and legs and thighs!

Old Man Winter
is really so unfair —
he hasn't left a bit of warmth
about me, anywhere!

February

The water's frozen on the pond;
It's thick from side to side.
Come out and help us clear the snow;
Get dressed, don't stay inside!

Half the town is meeting there,
So get your things and come.
We'll glide and swirl and crack the whip
Until our feet are numb. . .

Just one more race around the edge;
The sun is hanging low.
These winter days are much too short;
It's almost time to go!

March

"Brrr!" said the robin,
"I thought it was spring!
It's March, this I know,
And I'm ready to sing.
But my beak's nearly frozen,
My feet hardly move;
If this month is spring
Then I do not approve!"

March

The maple sap is running high.
Look, there's a slip of green!
The dogs are chasing crazily.
Is this a springtime scene?

The sun is bright and strangely warm.
What scents the breezes bring!
The drifts are melting off in streams.
Can it be … is it … spring?

The woods ring out with happy shouts.
A friendly robin sings.
A day like this can only mean
The springiest of springs!

April

April… still…
> until the wind wakens,
> tossing the trees in swirling dance.

April… still…
> until the clouds thicken,
> cracking the sky with sudden light.

April… still…
> until the rain rushes,
> drumming the roofs in reckless joy.

April… still…
> until the earth answers,
> filling the fields with newborn life.

April

April is tiptoeing into the land,
Touching each leaf with her delicate hand.

April is filling the air with a song;
Birds are returning, away for too long.

April is gentle and misty and cool,
Whispering dreams to the trees by the pool.

April's a girl in a long, flowing gown,
Wakening countryside, city and town.

May

Lilac-drenched morning, sweet gold of the day;
Tall tulips marching in jaunty array;
Blossoms unfolding, a brilliant display –
   Look! It's May!

Bird medleys chasing the stillness away;
Rustle of branches as fresh breezes play;
Starlings out building, no time for delay –
   Listen! It's May!

May

The apple trees wear blossom hats
On a spring-smile day in May.
White clouds drift on a sea of blue –
Shall I secretly sail away?

On a pink-blossom ship I could steer and soar
And never come back to this earth any more,
But land on a heavenly, star-lit shore . . .

The apple trees wear blossom hats
On this spring-smile day in May.
White clouds drift on a sea of blue;
Shall I secretly go – or stay?

June

Chirp, chirp, chirp is the song of June;
Hum, hum, hum swells the air;
Buzz, buzz, buzz from the flower hearts –
  June voices everywhere.

Gold, gold, gold shine the buttercups;
Blue, blue, blue is the sky;
Soft, soft, soft glow the mountain slopes –
  June colours fill the eye.

Bright, bright, bright, summer days begin;
Late, late, late, they depart;
Full, full, full are the hours of play –
  June gladness in your heart.

June

I just can't believe it –
It's happened at last!
School's finally ended,
The time really passed!

The last day is over,
The minutes ticked by.
The classroom is empty –
Hurray for July!

We're free for the summer,
The beach and the pool.
It's hello to baseball
And goodbye to school!

July

Picnic at noon, yellow balloon;
Building a castle of sand.
Sail on the bay, hours of play;
Running a lemonade stand.

Off on a trip, making stones skip;
Small-town parade with a band.
Strolling in parks, bonfire sparks –
Summer all over the land!

July

Lie on your front in the summer sand;
Bake for as long as you can stand.

Lie on your back, let the heat soak in;
Then roll around on your summer skin.

Lie on your side to enjoy the view;
Ease yourself over to toast side two.

Run to escape the blazing sun ...
It's too late – you're overdone!

August

A cricket
is piping out
his summer trill,
and I,
lying sleepless in the dark,
am wondering if
his grassy tent
is cool.

August

"Stop!" hissed the rain.
"You're spoiling my play!
I was here first —
it's my kind of day!"

"No!" huffed the wind.
"You stay in the sky!
Get back in the clouds —
it's time to be dry!"

"Wait!" blazed the sun.
"You don't have to fight!
It's my turn to choose —
this day will be bright!"

I don't know who won —
they bickered all day.
I was glad when the night
shooed them away.

September

As I walked to school today
A squirrel hurried by,
Fetching nuts to fill his store,
Too busy to be shy!

High above, I heard a sound,
The wild ducks' echoed call;
In the sky, a V-shaped sign
Announcing: Time for fall!

September

There are pickles and peppers and pumpkins and piecrusts;
Butter and ice cream and cheeses to share.
There are hot dogs and french fries and soft drinks and candy –
    How soon will we get to the fair?

There are tractors and balers and combines and seeders;
Hunters and Belgians and ponies to spare.
There's quilting and weaving and candles and sewing –
    How far is it now to the fair?

There's roping and shearing and milking and riding;
Roses and asters and orchids so rare.
There's bingo and skill games and fun and excitement –
    At last we've arrived at the fair!

October

Who has lightly touched the trees
And turned them all to flame,
With gold and brown and scarlet shades –
What is the painter's name?

Who has set the birds in flight?
Who has warned them all?
Who is bringing season's end?
Why, it must be Fall!

October

Sally, hi! I'm glad you came.
Boy, you sure don't look the same!

Sally, gee, I like your hat.
You look weird dressed up like that.

Sally, who'd believe the change?
Your face and hands are really strange.

Sally, that's a scary wig!
How'd you make your eyes so big?

Sally, wait! What did you say?

Sally? . . .

Gosh, she flew away!

November

The weatherman said, "Snow today,"
but children gazed in vain
for frosty snowflakes to be seen
beyond the window pane.

The weatherman said, "Snow tonight,
get out long underwear!"
But even though the children hoped,
the morning ground was bare.

The weatherman said, "Sun all day,
and clear until the dark."
By noon the sky was thick with snow
as winter left its mark!

November

Look at me, world! I'm almost complete;
They're bringing my scarf and my hat.
Gee, it's fantastic! I'm such a success,
So jolly and handsome and fat!

Stay with me, children! You know I'm just great;
My body's so sturdy and tall.
How can you leave me to stand by myself,
The most wonderful snowman of all?

Play with me, someone! Why there's Mr. Sun!
He sees that I'm dashing and bold;
He's looking and smiling so warmly at me.
That's great! Now I won't feel the cold!

December

It's poring over catalogues
And looking into stores;
It's dropping hints to Mom and Dad
And doing extra chores.

It's getting word to old St. Nick
In person or by mail;
It's peering under chests and beds
And mentioning a sale.

It's flutter-in-the-tummy time
And keeping on my toes;
It's trimming trees and counting days –
The Christmas feeling grows!

December

round slice of moon: December night
stark branches lift
from hollowed black to silvered white
          no wind disturbs

the stars swing by in frozen flight
soft smoke floats thin
from fires alight in rooms below
          the stillness holds

in silent snow
neat footprints write a winter's tale
          the night dreams on

Afterword

In recent years Canadian children have had more opportunities than ever before to see themselves and their country in their books. It is difficult, though, to think of a book that so completely evokes the environment and activities of Canadian children as does Sunflakes & Snowshine.

The traditional, anecdotal and quotable verses reflect the personality of each month of the year. The illustrations (reminiscent of both Van Gogh and Kurelek) have an originality, charm and humour all their own, and are satisfyingly child-like in their visual interpretations of the seasons. The book is genuinely on a child's level – simple, happy and unsophisticated – but it will also bring a warm feeling of nostalgia to many an adult heart and eye.

Sheila Egoff

Fran Newman and Claudette Boulanger met when Claudette's young daughter became a member of Fran's grade six class. The two became firm friends, and the happy result is Sunflakes & Snowshine.

Originally a Westerner, in 1970 Fran followed her airforce husband east, where she now lives with her family ("five kids, three cats, two dogs, three horses and fourteen chickens") on a farm near Frankford, Ontario. An enthusiastic and creative teacher, Fran brought her personal love for poetry to the classroom. The children's encouraging response persuaded her to begin writing verses of her own. Whether humorous or lyrical, Fran's poems are always sensitive to a child's feelings and point of view.

Recognizing a similar sensitivity to the world of childhood in the art of her friend, Fran proposed a "seasons" book that would capture the typical Canadian child's activities throughout the year. Claudette was delighted with the idea.

A graduate of the Alberta College of Art, Claudette is currently working in advertising. She has had a number of successful shows and has recently won two major awards: a National Award for Cartooning in the Public Interest in 1977, and a 1978 Award of Merit from the Art Directors Club of Toronto for the illustrations from Sunflakes & Snowshine. Claudette's interest in art began very early; she remembers frequent complaints from her teachers that she was always drawing when she should have been studying. Her unusual crayon work is particularly appealing to children, and Claudette considers her own three children her best — and harshest — critics.